# Pick of the Litter

By Teddy Slater
Illustrated by Carol Bouman and Dick Codor

A GOLDEN BOOK • NEW YORK
Western Publishing Company, Inc., Racine, Wisconsin 53404


Library of Congress Catalog Card Number: 85-81988 ISBN 0-307-02086-X
ISBN 0-307-60295-8 (lib. bdg.) C D E F G H I J

He had the same black muzzle, plumed tail, and button eyes as the other puppies in the litter. But it was his fuzzy little left ear that made him special. Instead of standing straight up like his right ear (and the ears of his brothers and sisters), it flopped down over his forehead.

Penny Pierpoint had never seen anything like it. He instantly stole her heart. "He looks just like a little bear," she cried. "I think I'll call him Grizzly."

"Now, Penny," her father warned, "don't get attached to these puppies. They're valuable show dogs, not pets. As soon as they're old enough, we'll sell them all."

"All but that one," said Penny's mother, glowering at Grizzly. "We'll be lucky if we can *give* him away!"

As time went by, the six puppies got bigger—and cuter. Penny couldn't help but love them.

One afternoon, Mrs. Pierpoint sold the biggest puppy. By the end of the week, only one pup remained—Grizzly. Penny worried and wondered when he, too, would be gone.

Penny was relieved when her mother finally declared, "Well, it seems no one wants this crooked-eared dog." If her parents couldn't find another home for Grizzly, Penny thought, they'd surely keep him for themselves.

But Penny's father added, "I guess we'll just have to take him to the pound."

Penny cried all the way to the pound, where she bade Grizzly a tearful good-by.

"Don't worry about that dog," Mr. Pierpoint said. "He'll make lots of new friends here."

"But I'll miss him," Penny wailed.

"You'll get over it," Mrs. Pierpoint said.

Penny didn't get over it. In fact, each day she missed Grizzly more. She felt as if she'd lost her best friend.

And it was all her parents' fault.

"They'll be sorry," Penny vowed as she packed her little suitcase. "I'll show them."

Back at the pound, Grizzly was lonesome for Penny.

But when he was taken to his new quarters, things seemed a little better. He was welcomed there by an amazing group of dogs, the Pound Puppies.

This group had one goal: finding homes for lost and stray pups.

The leader of the gang was Cooler.

"Let me introduce you to my friends, kid," he said to Grizzly. "They're the best doggone bunch of dogs you'll ever have the pleasure of meeting."

One by one, the Pound Puppies stepped forward to shake paws with Grizzly.

First there was Scrounger, the gang's Supply Chief. He had a knack for uncovering treasures in the unlikeliest places.

Next came The Nose, the puppies' Director of Information. She seemed to know everything that was going on inside and outside the pound.

And then there was Barkerville, the crew's Mission Coordinator. He did all the planning necessary for the placement of puppies in new homes.

Before long, Cooler and the gang had become a second family to Grizzly. But he still couldn't forget his "real" family.

It was The Nose who overheard the news in Pound Supervisor Bigelow's office. "Penny ran away from home early this morning," she told Grizzly. "The police and her parents have been searching for hours, but no one's seen or heard from her yet. They think she may be hurt or lost."

"I've got to find her," Grizzly cried, racing wildly around. "But first I've got to get out of here," he added after bouncing off the pound's locked door.

"No problem," Cooler replied. "I think I have a plan. We'll help you find your friend."

All the pups listened as Cooler outlined his idea.

"All right," he said when he'd finished explaining. "Scrounger, you get the catnip. Nose, you make sure Cat Gut gets a good whiff of Scrounger. Barkerville, you map out the route. And Grizzly, you make sure you're in the shower room at eight o'clock."

"This is kind of fun," Scrounger thought, rolling around in the catnip he'd filched from the Pound Supervisor's desk.

"Just in time," he thought as Supervisor Bigelow's mean cat, Cat Gut, came tearing down the hall, chased by The Nose. Huffing and puffing behind was Supervisor Bigelow.

"You leave that sweet little kitty alone, you mangy mutt," Bigelow threatened The Nose, "or I'll sock your big snoot."

Then Bigelow saw what Cat Gut was up to, and his jaw dropped open in amazement.

No cat had ever hated dogs more than Cat Gut. Yet there the cat was, rubbing up against Scrounger, purring blissfully, and trying to lick the scavenger's face.

"Get this creature off me," Scrounger howled.

"I just don't get it," Bigelow muttered in confusion. Then he spied the open tin of catnip on his desk.

"I'm not sure what you clowns are up to," Bigelow grumbled at the two dogs, "but I'm sure it's nothing good." Grabbing Scrounger by the collar, he snarled, "You come with me. You're getting a bath now, like it or not."

Scrounger pretended to put up a little fight. Everything was going according to schedule. In another minute he'd be in the shower room—exactly as planned.

Bigelow plopped Scrounger into the tub and started pouring soap flakes over him.

Grizzly arrived just as Cat Gut crept quietly into the shower room, nose twitching at Scrounger's catnip scent.

Cat Gut took a flying leap into the tub. Itchey and Snitchey, the pound guard dogs, got into the act. And then it was all hissing and spitting and biting!

While Bigelow struggled to get the soap out of his eyes, the Pound Puppies sprang into action. Cooler pried the grating off the big drainpipe in the middle of the floor. "Follow me," he cried, diving in.

Grizzly, The Nose, Barkerville, and Scrounger plunged after him.

Following Barkerville's map and Grizzly's hunch, the pups finally came up near a little pond just outside of town. The pond was in a park where Grizzly and Penny had spent many happy hours together.

And sure enough, there, under a big oak tree, was Penny.

She had fallen asleep in the afternoon sunshine, and had awakened to a dark, scary world. Afraid to stay and even more afraid to leave, she'd been sitting there for hours, not knowing what to do.

Grizzly gently licked the tears from her cheeks. Then he and his new friends took her home.

It was well past midnight when the Pierpoints returned from their search for Penny. They could hardly believe their eyes when they found her curled up on the living-room floor, fast asleep with her very best friend.

They woke Penny up and heard her story. And they decided to keep Grizzly in the family forever.

It was another job well done for the Pound Puppies!